CAT, YOU BETTER COME HOME

For Gregory, Terese, Rachel,
Nathan, and Aram, who know cats.
—G.K.

For Nasae, the Beast.
—S.J. and L.F.

CAT, YOU BETTER COME HOME

by Garrison Keillor

paintings by
Steve Johnson and Lou Fancher

PUFFIN BOOKS

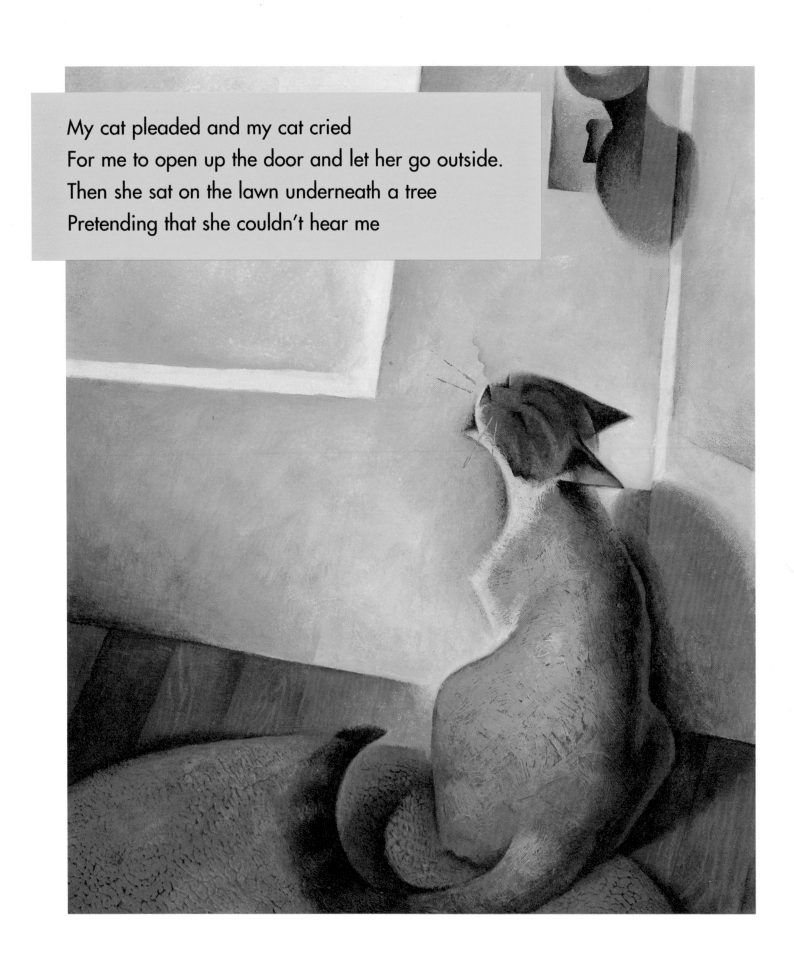

My cat pleaded and my cat cried
For me to open up the door and let her go outside.
Then she sat on the lawn underneath a tree
Pretending that she couldn't hear me

As I said, "CAT, YOU BETTER COME HOME!
There's dogs in the dark waiting to attack
And cat hawks looking for a late-night snack,
So CAT, YOU BETTER COME HOME."

Puff looked away and tossed her head—
"I may or may not come," she said.
"I'm a cat who is deeply dissatisfied.
I'll let you know when I decide."

I said, "CAT, YOU BETTER COME HOME.
I could close this door and lock the bolt
And you'd spend the night in the snow and cold,
So CAT, YOU BETTER COME HOME."

She said, "I'd rather be a cat who meets a terrible fate
Than live with a man who can't appreciate
That a cat is independent and a true highbrow
And needs a little high-class chow.

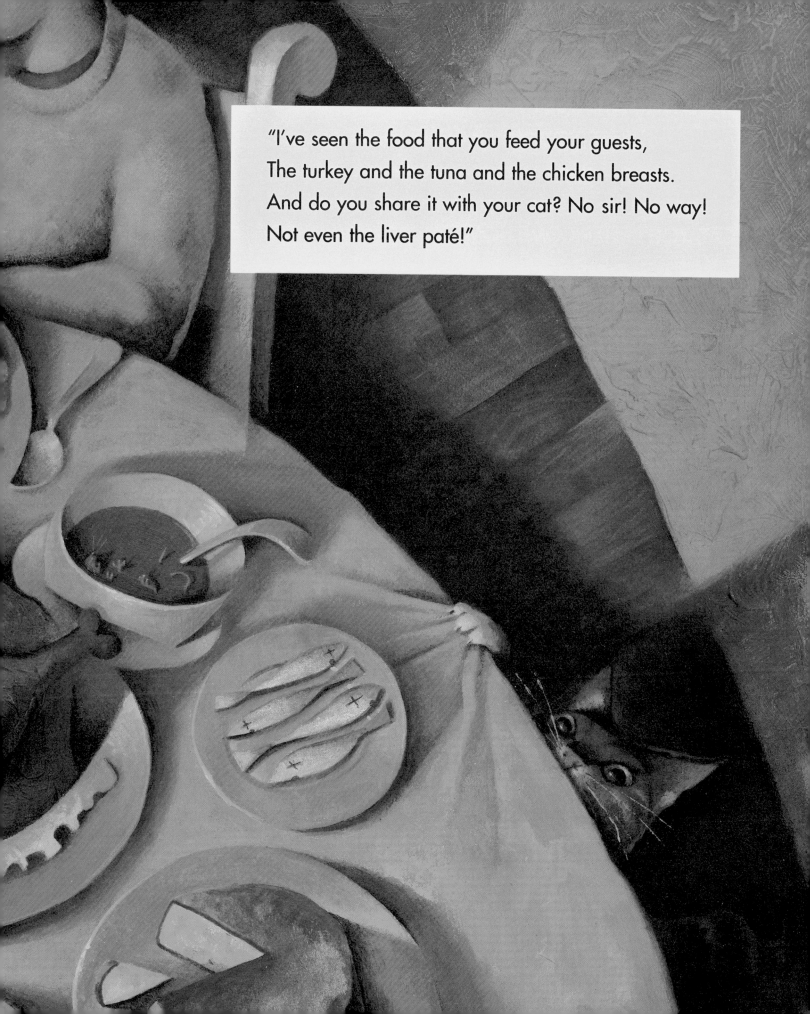

"I've seen the food that you feed your guests,
The turkey and the tuna and the chicken breasts.
And do you share it with your cat? No sir! No way!
Not even the liver paté!"

And I said, "CAT, YOU BETTER COME HOME.
I'm not about to stand here and argue with a cat!
What would the next-door neighbors think of that?
CAT, YOU BETTER COME HOME."

"*Well!* I never—" she said, and she turned in a huff.
"You've seen the last of your dear cat, Puff!"
She left with a *hmmph* and a sardonic laugh,
And she left for a year and a half.

I felt so bad, full of guilt and shame,
I walked around town, calling her name,
With a great big platter of Chateaubriand
And an ounce of caviar in my hand.

"O CAT, I WISH YOU'D COME HOME.
Come home, old Puff, come home to us,
There's a lot of new benefits I'd like to discuss.
O CAT, PLEASE COME HOME."

I saw her six months later in a cat magazine.
She was the Number One TV cat-food queen
With a fat contract with a cat-food firm,
And her hair was done up in a perm.

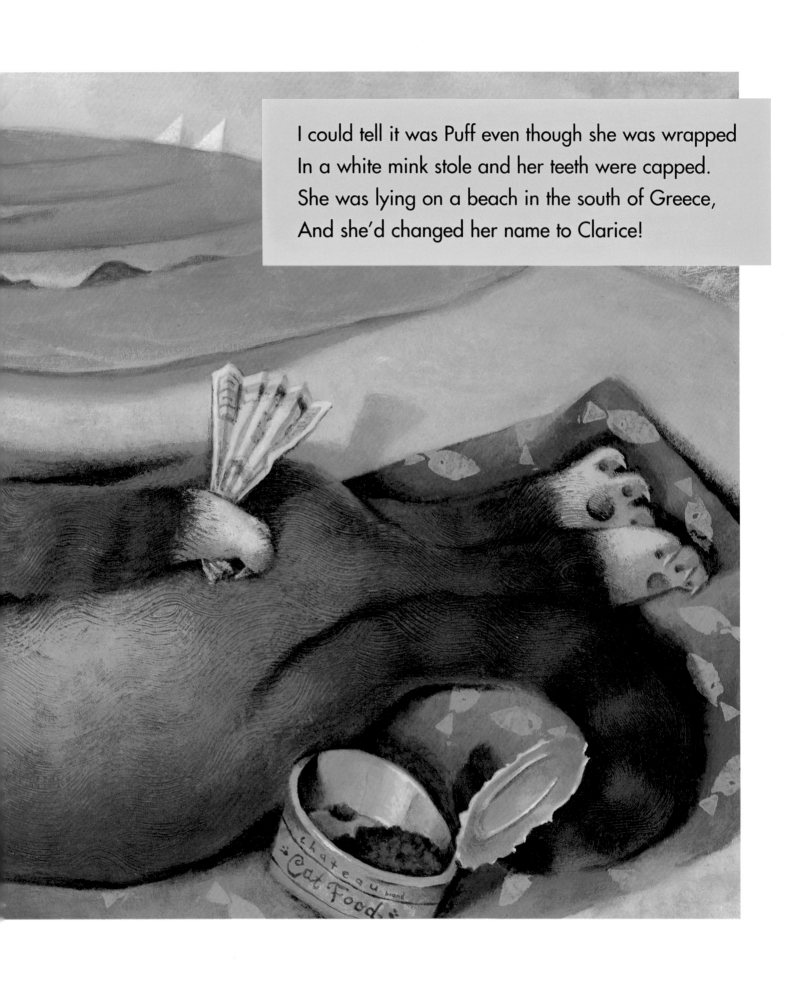

I could tell it was Puff even though she was wrapped
In a white mink stole and her teeth were capped.
She was lying on a beach in the south of Greece,
And she'd changed her name to Clarice!

In the story it said she was voted
Cat of All Cats by the Greeks, and it quoted
A noted poet who said, "Clarice
Is a national treasure and centerpiece."

And it said that she lived in a ten-room manse
And ate fresh fish flown in from France,
And that famous people visited her
And she spoke to them in a European purr!

"O CAT, YOU BETTER COME HOME!
You're no queen, you're Puff—you're *you*,
And your fans can't love you like your true friends do.
O CAT, YOU BETTER COME HOME."

She moved to a villa in Valenciennes,
And then to Copenhagen with a dog named Jens.
She had rich clothes, she had rich friends—
Her entourage was just immense:

Cooks and maids with long blonde braids,
A big brass band for her parades,
A string of minions to cringe and truckle,
Two comedians to make her chuckle,

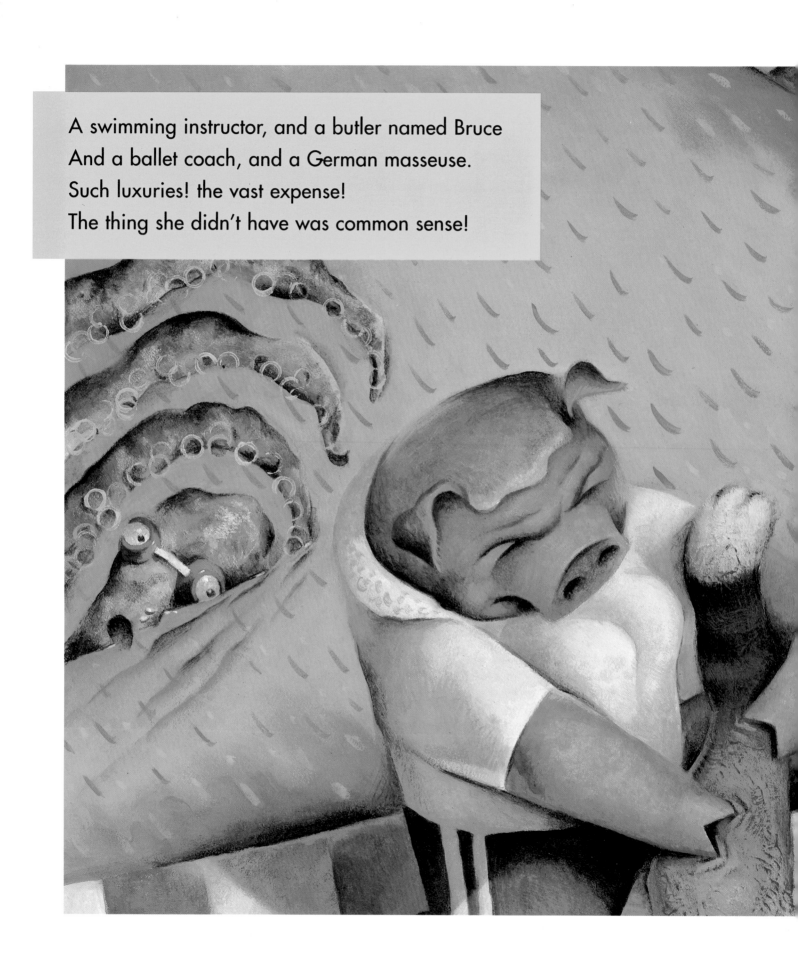

A swimming instructor, and a butler named Bruce
And a ballet coach, and a German masseuse.
Such luxuries! the vast expense!
The thing she didn't have was common sense!

She gave away gifts like she was St. Nicholas.
Her diamond bill was just ridicholas.

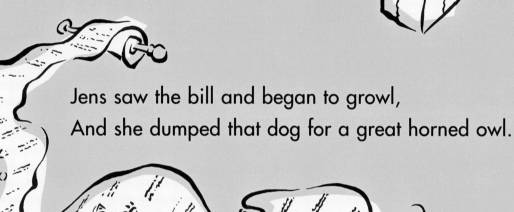

Jens saw the bill and began to growl,
And she dumped that dog for a great horned owl.

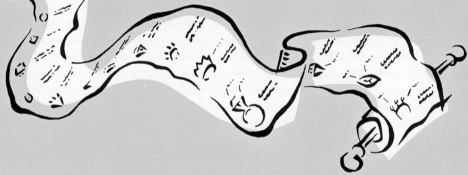

"O CAT, YOU BETTER COME HOME.
You're a top cat now and you're riding high
But they'll dump you in the river when the well runs dry,
So CAT, YOU BETTER COME HOME."

She spent a gazillion dollars on a yacht
Built in the shape of a flowerpot—
And nobody told her that a pot won't float,
So she sailed from Copenhagen with her owl dreamboat.
And the champagne popped, and the music played,
And the people clapped on the promenade,

And the boat went *bloop*, and the owl cried *Hoooo*,
And Puff cried *No!* and the owl flew
As the boat sank *blubblubblubblubssssssssss*
And the cat went down in the watery abyss.

Everyone stood by the waterside
And watched the bubbles and softly cried,
"O darling cat, O angel flower,"
And a team of divers dove for an hour.

And when it got too sad to watch 'em,
They hung out a sign, *Requiescat pacem*,
And went to a feast at Le Café Triste,
Assuming the beast was at least deceased.

And that was the last I heard, until,
Early one morning when the house was still,
Came a *scratch-scratch-scratch* from the windowsill,

And there with her nose pressed against the pane,
Burrs in her fur, and drenched from the rain,
With tears in her ears and big puffy eyelids,
Stood a former top cat who had hit the skids.

She limped along on a homemade crutch.
She could hardly stand, she weighed so much—
Approximately ninety-three pounds.

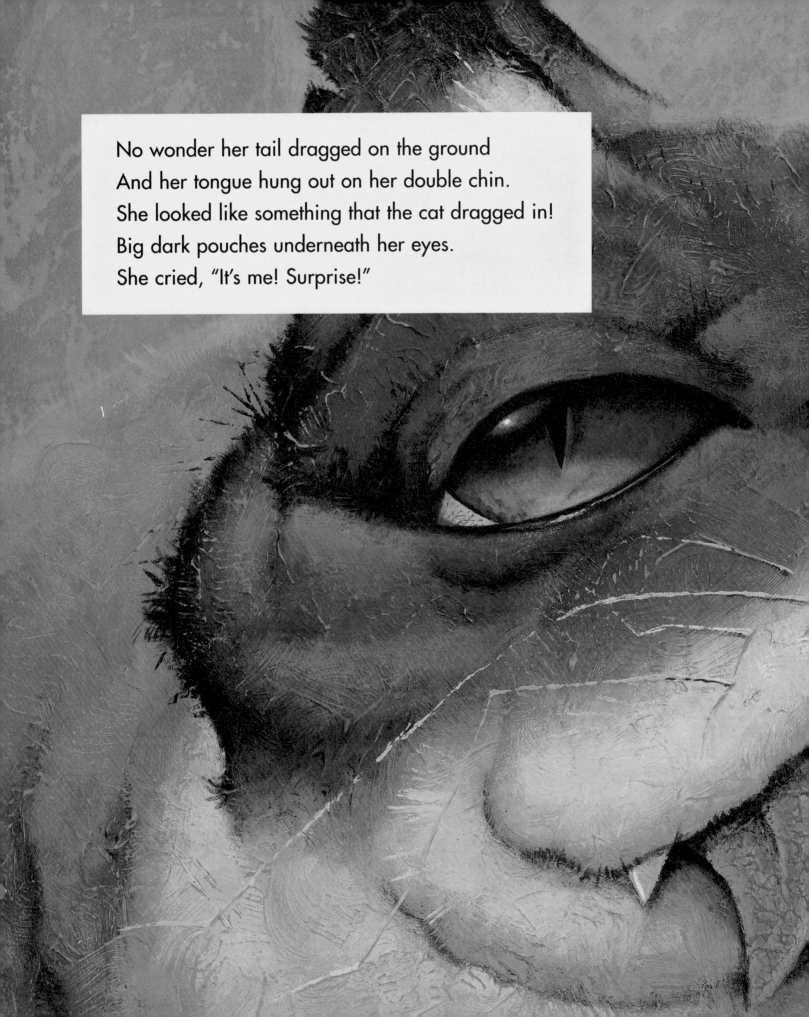

No wonder her tail dragged on the ground
And her tongue hung out on her double chin.
She looked like something that the cat dragged in!
Big dark pouches underneath her eyes.
She cried, "It's me! Surprise!"

"O CAT, I'M GLAD YOU CAME HOME!
No need to explain, my old cat friend,
I'm just glad to have you back again.
YES CAT, I'M SO GLAD YOU CAME HOME!"

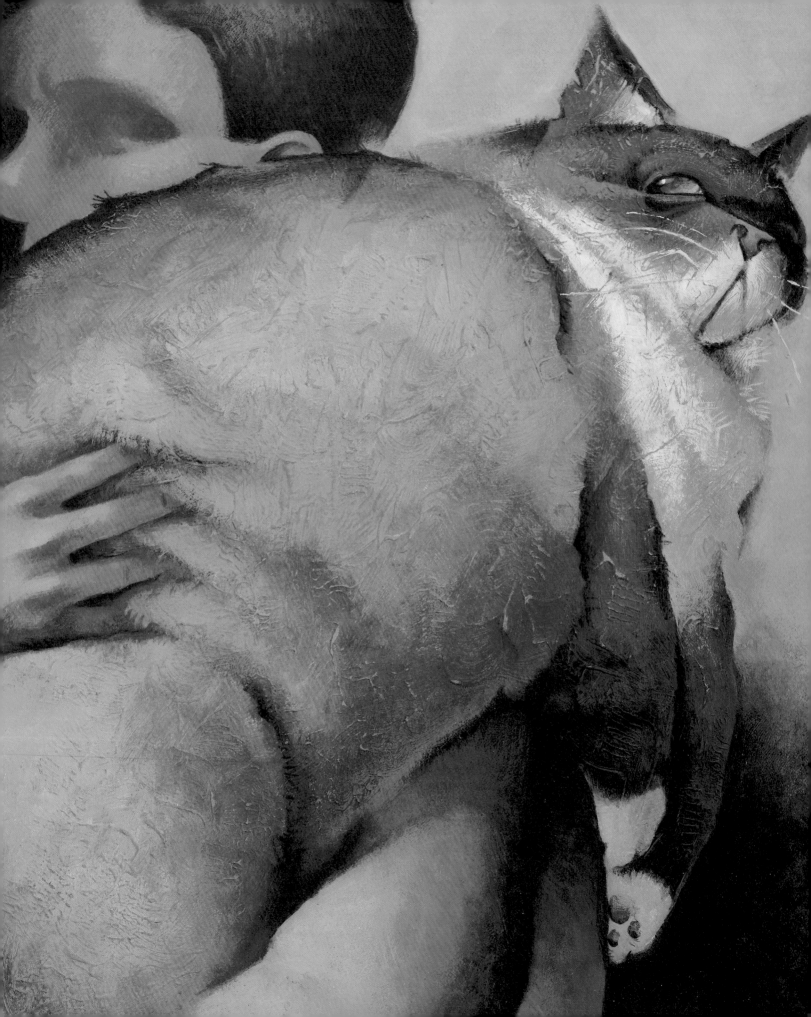

I picked her up, my old fur sack—
She cried, "Easy, Jack, take it easy on my back.
I've got bad back problems and I'm not too swift,
On account of the rich, rich life I've lived.
I'm gonna give up gravy and goldfish pies,
Ragout of robin thighs,

Guppy fries and frog fillet,
Mouse morsels served flambé,

White rats in chocolate sauce,
Soup *à la* collie paws,

Chihuahuas in cheddar cheese,
Chuck roast of chickadees,

And one more thing—I know it well!—
A cat should never drink muscatel."

She went on a high-fiber diet at once
And was her old self in about two months.
With a spring in her step and a gleam in her eye,
She'd hop to the windowsill, sit there, and sigh,

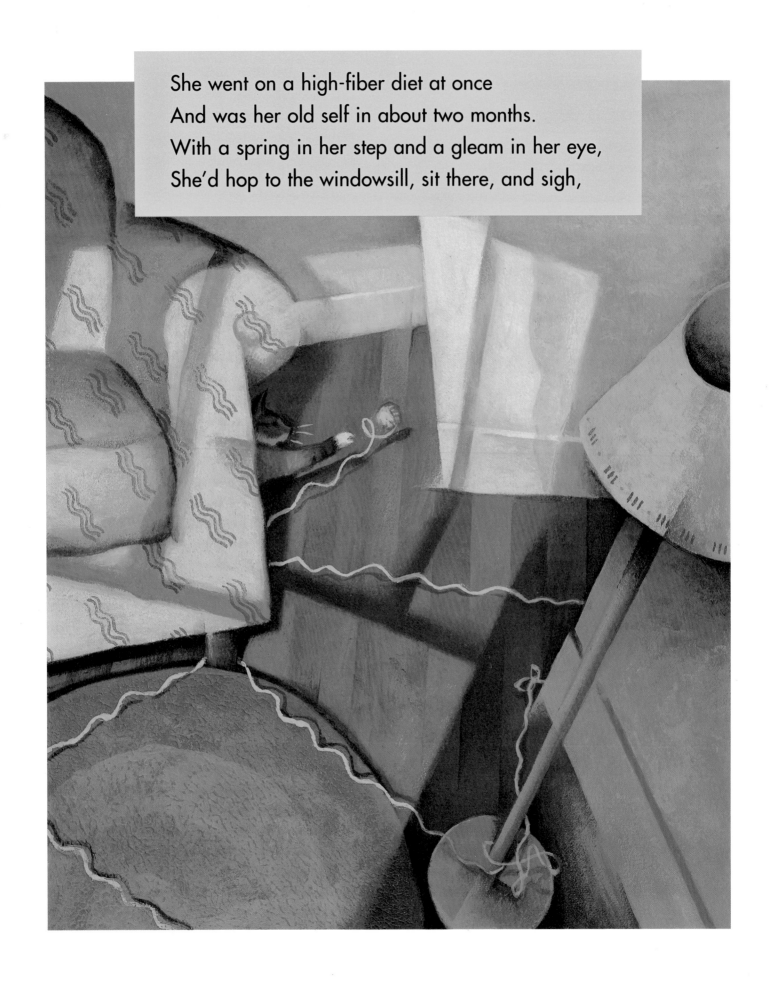

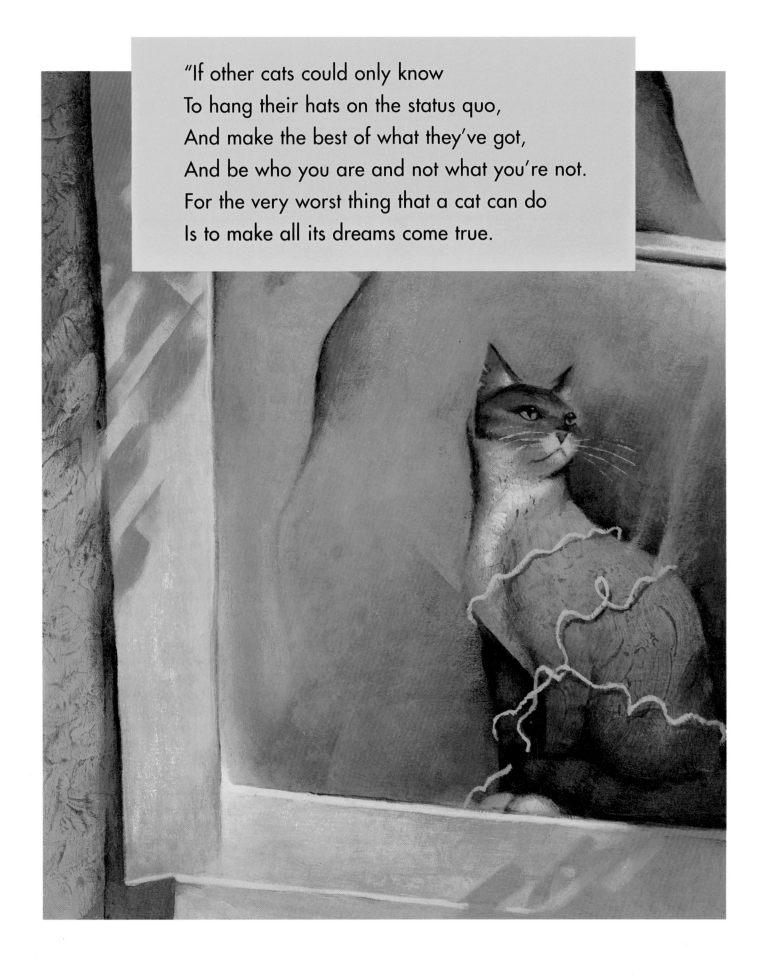

"If other cats could only know
To hang their hats on the status quo,
And make the best of what they've got,
And be who you are and not what you're not.
For the very worst thing that a cat can do
Is to make all its dreams come true.

"So CATS, YOU BETTER COME HOME.
You can seek your fortune, but nevertheless,
Remember your name and your address,
Because someday YOU'LL NEED TO COME HOME."

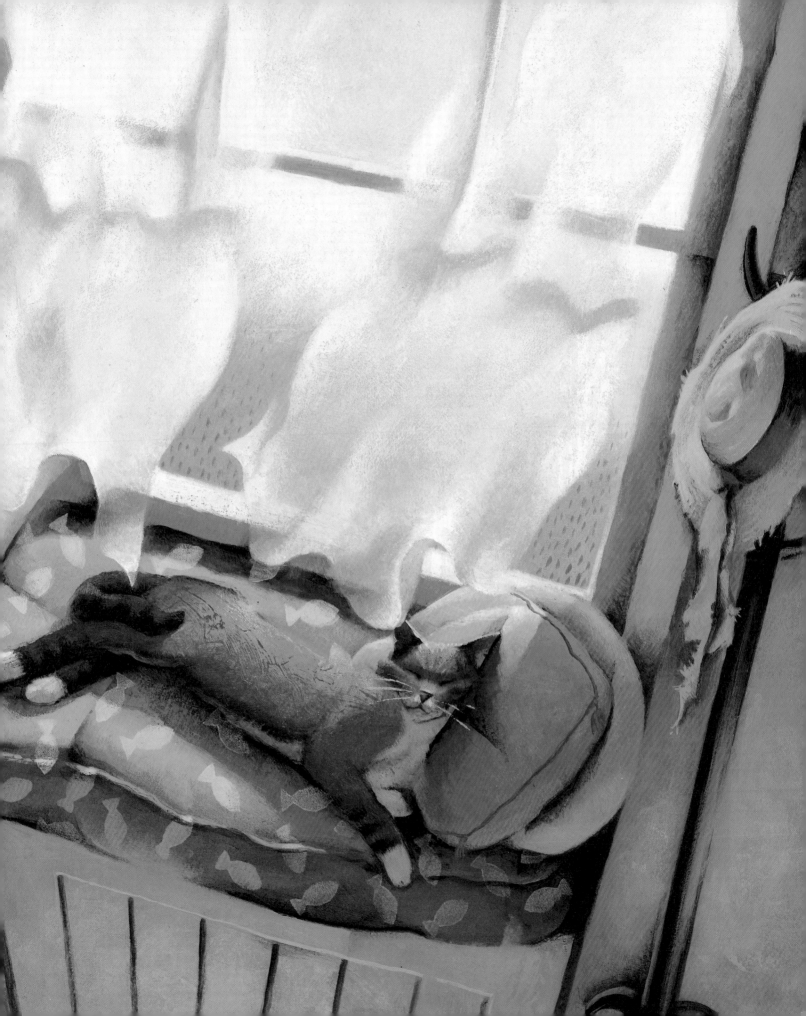

PUFFIN BOOKS
Published by the Penguin Group
Penguin Books USA Inc., 375 Hudson Street,
New York, New York 10014, U.S.A.
Penguin Books Ltd, 27 Wrights Lane, London W8 5TZ, England
Penguin Books Australia Ltd, Ringwood, Victoria, Australia
Penguin Books Canada Ltd, 10 Alcorn Avenue, Toronto,
Ontario, Canada M4V 3B2
Penguin Books (N.Z.) Ltd, 182-190 Wairau Road,
Auckland 10, New Zealand

Penguin Books Ltd, Registered Offices:
Harmondsworth, Middlesex, England

First published in the United States of America by Viking,
a division of Penguin Books USA Inc., 1995
Published in Puffin Books, 1997

1 3 5 7 9 10 8 6 4 2

THE LIBRARY OF CONGRESS HAS CATALOGED THE VIKING EDITION AS FOLLOWS:
Keillor, Garrison. Cat, you better come home / by Garrison Keillor;
paintings by Steve Johnson and Lou Fancher. p. cm.
Summary: Dissatisfied with her life, Puff the cat leaves home
and becomes a rich and glamorous model, but eventually returns
having found out that it's better to be who you are.
ISBN 0-670-85112-4
[1. Cats—Fiction. 2. Stories in rhyme.] I. Johnson, Steve, ill.
II. Fancher, Lou, ill. III. Title.
PZ8.3.K27Cat 1995 [E]—dc20 94-39230 CIP AC

Puffin Books ISBN 0-14-056227-3

This story is a revised version of Garrison Keillor's poem
"Cat, You Better Come Home," which was recorded by the author for
the audiocassette titled "Song of the Cat" (distributed by Penguin HighBridge),
copyright © Garrison Keillor, 1991.

Printed in the United States of America